To Lena, my little bean
Special thanks to Lee
—K. K.

Margaret K. McElderry Books
An imprint of Simon & Schuster Children's
Publishing Division
1230 Avenue of the Americas
New York, NY 10020

Book design by Lee Wade
The text of this book is set in Venetian.
The illustrations are rendered in collage,
gouache, and colored pencils.
Manufactured in China

Library of Congress Catalog Card Number: 00-103345
ISBN-13: 978-1-4169-7502-1
ISBN-10: 1-4169-7502-0

counting kisses

by karen katz

MARGARET K. McELDERRY BOOKS
NEW YORK LONDON TORONTO SYDNEY

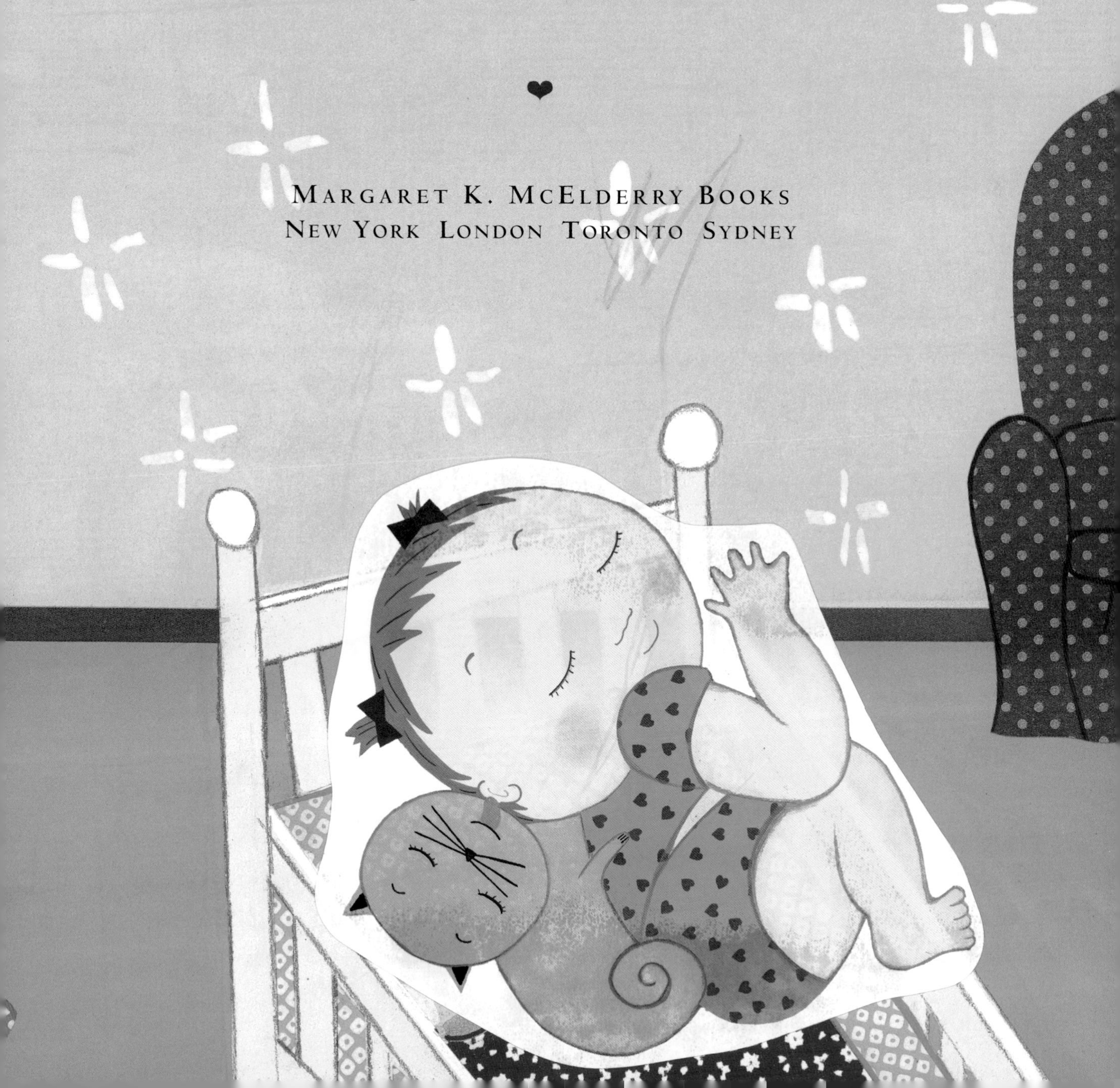

My tired
little baby,
do you need
a kiss?

ten

little kisses on
teeny tiny toes

❤ ❤ ❤ ❤ ❤ ❤ ❤ ❤ ❤ ❤

nine

laughing kisses
on busy, wriggly feet

❤ ❤ ❤ ❤ ❤ ❤ ❤ ❤ ❤

9

eight

squishy kisses on
chubby, yummy knees

8

seven loud kisses on a pretty

belly button ❤ ❤ ❤ ❤ ❤ ❤ ❤ 7

six

tickly kisses on
baby's dimpled chin

five

quick kisses on
an itty bitty nose

❤ ❤ ❤ ❤ ❤

four

warm kisses on
two baby hands

❤ ❤ ❤ ❤

three

fuzzy kisses on
sweet little ears

❤ ❤ ❤

3

two gentle kisses on tired

closing eyes. ❤ ❤ 2

one

last kiss on your sleepy, dreamy head

❤

1

for baby's
bed.